Sneaky
Short cut

For Dudley D. Watkins ~

First published in hardback in Great Britain by Andersen Press Ltd in 1996
First published in paperback by Picture Lions in 1998
This edition published by Collins Picture Books in 2002

5 7 9 10 8 6 4
ISBN-13: 978-0-00-714015-2
ISBN-10: 0-00-714015-0

Picture Lions and Collins Picture Books are imprints of the Children's Division, part of HarperCollins Publishers Ltd.
Text and illustrations copyright © Colin McNaughton 1996
The author/illustrator asserts the moral right to be identified as the author/illustrator of the work.
A CIP catalogue record for this title is available from the British Library.

Vist our website at: www.harpercollinschildrensbooks.co.uk

Printed in Hong Kong

Colin McNaughton

Oops!

HarperCollins *Children's Books*

It was the same old story.
Mister Wolf was hungry.
Mister Wolf was very hungry
and Mister Wolf had his
eye on Preston Pig.

Mister Wolf was hungry
for three very good reasons:

1. Mister Plimp the shopkeeper
had banned him from his shop
for eating the customers.

2. Mister Plump the park keeper
had banned him from the park
for picnicking on the visitors.

3. Miss Thump the school
teacher had banned him
from the school grounds
for snacking on the students.

"Don't look at me like that,
I'm the Big Bad Wolf!
It's my job to be nasty.
These stories would be
pretty boring if I was
good, wouldn't they?"

Suddenly!

There was a huge crash.
"Oops!" said Preston.

Oops!

"You clumsy great pudding!" said Preston's mum. "Get out from under my feet and take that basket of food to your granny's. She's not well."

"Yes, Mum," said Preston.

"And tell Granny I'll be over later to chop her some wood," said Preston's dad.

"Yes, Dad," said Preston.

"And put your coat on," said Preston's mum.

"Yes, Mum," said Preston.

"And don't slam the door," said Preston's dad. "The chimney pot is loose…"

"Slam!" went the door.
"Oops!" went Preston.

"Hmm…red hood, basket of food, granny's house? That reminds me of a story, but which one?" said Mister Wolf – just before the chimney pot landed on his head.

Oops!

"I know it isn't *The Three Little Pigs*," said Mister Wolf. "But I do like that story. Especially the bit where the wolf eats the three little pigs and escapes. Well, that's how *my* mum used to tell it!"

Mister Wolf tried some cunning
wolf tricks to catch Preston
but he didn't have much luck.

Cunning Wolf Trick No. 1
The old 'Banana Skin' ploy.

Cunning Wolf Trick No. 2
The old 'Dig-a-Deep-Pit' dodge.

Cunning Wolf Trick No. 3
The old 'If-All-Else-Fails-Bash-'em-on-the-Head-with-a-Big-Stick' plan.

Preston reached Granny's house safely. Mister Wolf was fed up. He was hot and sticky, scratched, stung and bitten. "And I still can't remember that rotten story!" said Mister Wolf.

Suddenly!

There was a huge crash.
"Oops!" said Preston.

Mister Wolf sneaked up
to the window and this
is what he heard…

"What big eyes you've got,
Granny!" said Preston.
"All the better to see you
smash my teapot!" said Granny.

"What big ears you've got,
Granny!" said Preston.
"All the better to hear you
smash my cups!" said Granny.

"What big teeth you've got,
Granny!" said Preston.
"All the better to gnash
when you smash my sugar
bowl!" said Granny.

"Hey!" cried Mister Wolf, "those are *my* lines! I remember that story now. It's *Little Red Riding Hood*." Mister Wolf leaped through the window, tied Granny up and stuffed Preston in a sack.

"Now, let me think," said Mister Wolf. "How does that story end?" He was just opening the door when he remembered…

"Oops!"
said Mister Wolf.

Collect all the Preston Pig Stories

Colin McNaughton
Suddenly!
Look behind you, Preston Pig!
0-00-714013-4

Colin McNaughton
GOAL!
Go football crazy with Preston Pig!
0-00-714011-8

Colin McNaughton
BOO!
Surprise! It's Preston Pig!
0-00-714014-2

Colin McNaughton
Oops!
I'm coming to get you, Preston Pig!
0-00-714015-0

Colin McNaughton
Shh!
(Don't Tell Mister Wolf)
A Preston Pig Lift-the-Flap Book
0-00-664715-4

Colin McNaughton
Hmm...
Who's hungry for Preston Pig?
0-00-714012-6

Colin McNaughton
Oomph!
Fall in love with Preston Pig!
0-00-712635-2

Colin McNaughton
little Suddenly!
a Preston Pig toddler book
0-00-713235-2

Colin McNaughton
little Oops!
a Preston Pig toddler book
0-00-713236-0

Colin McNaughton
little Goal!
a Preston Pig toddler book
0-00-713234-4

Colin McNaughton
little Boo!
a Preston Pig toddler book
0-00-713237-9

Colin McNaughton
WHEE!
A Preston Pig TV Story
0-00-712371-X

Colin McNaughton
POOH!
A Preston Pig TV Story
0-00-712370-1

Colin McNaughton
PARP!
A Preston Pig TV Story
0-00-712372-8

Colin McNaughton is one of Britain's most highly-acclaimed picture book talents and a winner of many prestigious awards. His Preston Pig Stories are hugely successful with Preston now starring in his own animated television series on CITV.